# THE SINGING SERPENTS

TAHIR SHAH

OKSANA MYCHKA-MAYLONE

# THE SINGING SERPENTS

*A Teaching Story*

TAHIR SHAH

OKSANA MYCHKA-MAYLONE

MMXXIV

Secretum Mundi Publishing Ltd
124 City Road
London
EC1V 2NX
United Kingdom

www.secretum-mundi.com
info@secretum-mundi.com

First published by Secretum Mundi Publishing Ltd, 2024
A version of this story originally appeared in *Scorpion Soup* by Tahir Shah, 2013

THE SINGING SERPENTS



Artwork drawn by Oksana Mychka-Maylone



A CIP catalogue record for this title is available from the British Library.

ISBN 978-1-915876-06-5

VERSION 18072023

Visit the author's website:
Tahirshah.com

When a crow sings the song of a nightingale,
it will be a nightingale and no longer a crow.

*Indian saying*

## Teaching Stories

When I was small, I was told stories from morning till night.

I was told stories about genies and witches and about great birds that could carry away elephants on their wings… and stories about distant kingdoms and magical lands ruled by warrior kings.

I was told stories of good and bad… stories of hope and others of despair.

I was even told stories about stories.

And all the while, I listened, amazed.

The more I listened, the more my mind worked… and the more I came to understand that these stories had a power about them, a secret lifeblood all of their own.

They were magical instruments, machineries that could alter states of mind and change the way we think.

But most importantly of all, stories can teach us, without us realizing that they are doing so at all.

Part of the default programming of man, stories are within us all.

Born into us, they make us who we are – they make us human.

Since earliest childhood, I have feasted on stories as a way of learning about the world, and learning about myself. They have been my dictionary and my encyclopaedia, my classroom, my guide, and my very best friend.

To descend down through the layers of stories is to be reborn, into a dominion of fantasy – one touched by real magic.

Pre-eminent within the great treasuries of tales, it is teaching stories like this one that have shown me the path to follow beyond the next horizon, and have made me the man I am.

Tahir Shah

Once upon a time, there lived in Arabia an especially wise cat.

This wise cat always had enough to eat and drink, and was pampered by his human masters.

But he dreamed of something else.

He dreamed of something magical to
inspire him, something to warm his heart.

The other cats thought he was senseless.

They told him to remain quiet, to live his life
as they all did, being looked after by man.

‘We have existed like this for thousands of years,’ they told him, ‘and we are very good at it.

‘We have the lifestyle perfected – a lifestyle in which humans give us plenty of food and attention, and in which we need to provide almost nothing in return.’

But the wise cat didn’t listen to them.

He knew that the only thing that mattered in life was to make his own path – a path that the foolish cats didn't realize existed at all.

So the wise cat packed a knapsack
and set off in search of his destiny.

Within minutes of his departure, all the other cats had forgotten about him. They went back to their chunks of juicy meat, to their big bowls of milk, and to the attentions of mankind.

The wise cat travelled from one kingdom to the next, learning languages and immersing himself in different lands. And with each day that passed, the wise cat became all the wiser.

Now, one day, the cat reached
a country ruled by dogs.

There were big gruff dogs,
little yapping dogs, dogs that were kind
to cats… and others that were not.

With no other cats there at all, the wise cat had no choice but to spend his time with the dogs.

He found them to be quite easy-going and far less complicated than his own species.

Dogs, as he reasoned it,
were all bark and no bite.

There was nothing that got the dogs worked up… nothing except the subject of singing snakes.

The mere mention of the reptiles threw every dog in the kingdom into a wild frenzy of fear and reaction.

‘Singing snakes come in the night and swallow you whole,’ one of the dogs told him.

‘They’ve got teeth like knitting needles,’ another revealed.

'They hypnotize you with their eyes and there's nothing you can do to break free!' exclaimed a third.

The wise cat listened to the dogs.

When they were finished, he asked: 'Have any of you dogs ever seen a singing snake?'

The dogs shielded their eyes with
their paws in terror.
'No, no, of course not,' they howled.

‘So how do you know that you are really afraid of them?’ asked the cat.

Standing on hind legs, the smallest dog, a Pomeranian, said: ‘Because we all know that we are, and that’s that!’

A few weeks passed, and the wise cat lived quietly among the dogs. He was always polite and the majority of the dogs treated him well.

From time to time he was chased,
but mostly the dogs left him alone.

Instead of disliking him, they regarded him as something of a novelty.

Then, one night, an elderly dog had a dream.

Or rather, it was a nightmare.

He dreamed that a plague of singing serpents was about to strike – a race of evil reptiles dead set on swallowing every single dog whole.

Word of his dream spread like wildfire and, as it did so, the entire community was thrown into disarray.

‘What are we going to do?’ yelped the dogs. ‘We are powerless. The singing snakes will swallow us whole!’

Sitting on a fence in the middle of the town,
the wise cat listened to the fuss.

He watched as the normally level-headed dogs worked themselves into a frenzy about an old dog's ludicrous dream.

By the afternoon, the dogs were digging holes on a large scale – holes to hide in when the singing-snake invasion took place.

After that, they convened an emergency council in their great hall, at which all dogs were invited to debate the worrying state of affairs.

As he was the only cat in the kingdom,
the wise cat was allowed to come along.

He listened to the many speeches, all of them tinged with hysteria and fear. And he watched as the canine community grew ever more agitated.

By the end of the evening, he could stand it no more and jumped up onto the podium.

'I may be just a cat,' he said, 'but that gives me an advantage.'

The dogs looked confused.
'What is it – your advantage?' they barked.

‘It is that I can see your situation from the outside, while you can only see it from within.’

‘So what?’ snapped the dogs.

‘Well, it means that I can see how to solve your problem.’

A cluster of dogs at the front of the hall began barking ferociously.

'Tell the cat to get out!' they growled.
'This is dog business!'

But the old dog that had dreamed the dream in the first place called for hush. 'Let the cat speak,' he snarled.

So the wise cat continued:
'Because I am not one of you, I have been able to watch you with detachment,' he said, 'and I've seen that you dogs are easy-going.

‘But…’ the cat paused to take in his audience, ‘the idea of singing serpents has thrown your lives upside down. Why is that?’

'Because serpents swallow dogs whole!'
barked a chihuahua anxiously at the back.
'And every dog alive knows that!'

‘Let me ask a question,’ replied the wise cat. ‘How many of you have ever seen a singing serpent?’

There was silence.

Then, a Labrador pointed at the old dog.
'*He* has,' he yelped. 'Old Dog has seen one,
in his dream!'

The wise cat smiled demurely.
'In his dream...?'

A wave of murmuring swept through the room. The dogs didn't like the idea of a cat – however wise – trying to make fun of them.

But mockery was not on the cat's mind.

Rather, he raised a paw very slowly and said: 'My dear dog friends, good fortune smiles on your community. You see, as chance would have it, I was sold something in the next kingdom, something very precious and very powerful…

'… something that can protect us all
from the singing snakes.'

‘What is it? What is it?!’
barked the dogs anxiously.

The wise cat held something above his head.

Something very small and shiny.

Craning forwards, the dogs were desperate to know what it was. They clambered over each other, eyes wide, mouths drooling, noses sniffing.

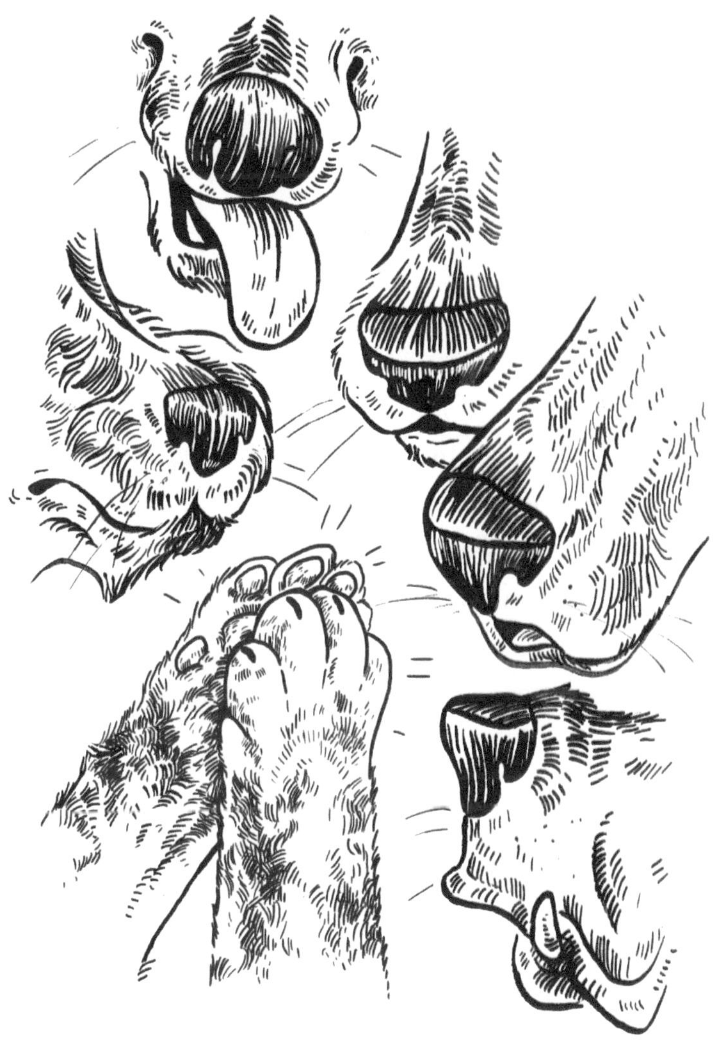

‘This is an amulet of awe-inspiring power!’ exclaimed the wise cat. ‘It was made by a famous magician to protect its owner from the danger of singing serpents!’

The dogs gasped.
They yelped.
Some howled.

All were relieved.

'You dogs have been good to me,' the wise cat said, 'and so I am presenting the amulet to you all as a gift – a gift of my affection!'

‘We’ll make a special shrine for it!’
yelped a spaniel.

‘We’ll guard it and look after it!’
growled another poodle.

‘We will devote our lives to it!’
barked a terrier.

The cat seemed pleased.

Jumping down from the podium,
he passed the sacred amulet to the old dog.

‘Make sure you protect it,’ he said.

Then he left.

Clustering around, each of the dogs gave thanks to the wise cat for saving them from the invasion of the singing snakes – an invasion that was thwarted at the last moment…

… by nothing more than
an ordinary metal button.

*Finis*

## *About the Author*

Descended from a long line of storytellers, writers, and savants, Tahir Shah is one of the most prolific authors of his generation. He has published more than sixty books in numerous genres, including travel, fiction, and fantasy, as well as tales for children.

Raised in the tradition of Eastern 'teaching stories', Shah is passionate about stories and storytelling. He regards the ability to learn from folklore as being in us all, what he calls a 'default setting of humankind'. As well as having written scores of books, Shah has made documentaries for National Geographic TV and The History Channel. He is the founder and CEO of the charity, The Scheherazade Foundation.

## *About the Artist*

Oksana Mychka-Maylone is a Ukrainian artist born and bred in the cultural heart of Lviv. She has always been captivated by the allure of books and the intricacies of their creation, choosing to dedicate her life to studying the process. After completing her studies and earning a master's degree in imprint graphics (linorite, lithography, and etching), Oksana delved into the world of traditional ink illustration, drawing inspiration from the breathtaking landscapes of her native Carpathian Mountains and the rich tapestry of Ukrainian folklore.

Now residing in the United States, she continues to express her passion for the art of book creation and illustration.

*Books By Tahir Shah*

*The Writer's Craft*

The Reason to Write

Workbook: Comprehensive, Volume I & II

Workbook: Fantasy, Volume I & II

Workbook: Fiction, Volume I & II

Workbook: Historical Fiction, Volume I & II

Workbook: Teaching Stories, Volume I & II

Workbook: Travel, Volume I & II

*Novels*

Jinn Hunter: Book One – The Prism

Jinn Hunter: Book Two – The Jinnslayer

Jinn Hunter: Book Three – The Perplexity

Hannibal Fogg and the Supreme Secret of Man

Casablanca Blues

Eye Spy

Godman

Paris Syndrome

Timbuctoo

Midas

Zigzagzone

*Nasrudin*

Travels With Nasrudin

The Misadventures of the Mystifying Nasrudin

The Peregrinations of the Perplexing Nasrudin

The Voyages and Vicissitudes of Nasrudin

Nasrudin in the Land of Fools

*Travel*

Trail of Feathers

Travels With Myself

Beyond the Devil's Teeth

In Search of King Solomon's Mines

House of the Tiger King

In Arabian Nights

The Caliph's House

Sorcerer's Apprentice

Journey Through Namibia

*Teaching Stories*

The Arabian Nights Adventures

Scorpion Soup

Tales Told to a Melon

The Afghan Notebook

Daydreams of an Octopus & Other Stories

The Caravanserai Stories

Ghoul Brothers

Hourglass

Imaginist

Jinn's Treasure

Jinnlore

Mellified Man

Skeleton Island

Wellspring

When the Sun Forgot to Rise

Outrunning the Reaper

The Cap of Invisibility

On Backgammon Time

The Wondrous Seed

The Paradise Tree
Mouse House
The Hoopoe's Flight
The Old Wind
A Treasury of Tales
The Tale of Double Six
The Forgotten Game
King of the Jinns
The Destiny Ring
Changing the World
Cat, Mouse
Frogland
Mittle-Mittle
Capilongo
The Princess of Zilzilam
The Singing Serpents
The Tale of the Rusty Nail
The Unicorn's Tear
The Clockmaker Who Travelled Through Time
The Fish's Dream
The Man Whose Arms Grew Branches
The Most Foolish of Men
The Shop That Sold Truth
Qwerty
Renaissance
The Man With the Tiger's Head
The Kingdom of Blink
The Wisdom of Celestine
Dream Soup
The Skeleton Factory
An Unexpected Gift

The Problem Exchange
The Pharaoh Code
The Monkey Puzzle Club
Liquid Time
Cat Dog, Dog Cat
Princess Pickle's Laugh

*Anthologies*

The Anthologies: Africa
The Anthologies: Ceremony
The Anthologies: Childhood
The Anthologies: City
The Anthologies: Danger
The Anthologies: East
The Anthologies: Expedition
The Anthologies: Frontier
The Anthologies: Hinterland
The Anthologies: India
The Anthologies: Jinns
The Anthologies: Jungle
The Anthologies: Magic
The Anthologies: Morocco
The Anthologies: Nasrudin
The Anthologies: People
The Anthologies: Quest
The Anthologies: South
The Anthologies: Taboo
The Anthologies: Teaching Stories
The Clockmaker's Box
The Tahir Shah Fiction Reader
The Tahir Shah Travel Reader

*Research*

Cultural Research

The Middle East Bedside Book

Three Essays

*Edited by*

Congress With a Crocodile

A Son of a Son, Volume I

A Son of a Son, Volume II

*Screenplays*

Casablanca Blues: The Screenplay

Timbuctoo: The Screenplay

## A REQUEST

If you enjoyed this book, please review it on your favourite online retailer or review website.

**Reviews are an author's best friend.**

To stay in touch with Tahir Shah, and to hear about his upcoming releases before anyone else, please sign up for his mailing list:

 http://tahirshah.com/newsletter

And to follow him on social media, please go to any of the following links:

 http://www.twitter.com/humanstew

 @tahirshah999

 http://www.facebook.com/TahirShahAuthor

 http://www.youtube.com/user/tahirshah999

 http://www.pinterest.com/tahirshah

 https://www.goodreads.com/tahirshahauthor

**http://www.tahirshah.com**

www.ingramcontent.com/pod-product-compliance
Lightning Source LLC
Chambersburg PA
CBHW030523310726
48979CB00010B/1774/J

* 9 7 8 1 9 1 5 8 7 6 0 6 5 *